ReadZone Books Limited

50 Godfrey Avenue
Twickenham
TW2 7PF
UK

© ReadZone Books 2014
© in text Jillian Powell 2004
© in illustrations Tim Archbold 2004

Jillian Powell has asserted her right under the Copyright Designs and Patents Act 1988
to be identified as the author of this work.

Tim Archbold has asserted his right under the Copyright Designs and Patents Act 1988
to be identified as the illustrator of this work.

First published in this edition by Evans Brothers Ltd, London in 2010.

Every attempt has been made by the Publisher to secure appropriate permissions for material
reproduced in this book. If there has been any oversight we will be happy to rectify the situation
in future editions or reprints. Written submissions should be made to the Publisher.

British Library Cataloguing in Publication Data (CIP) is available for this title.

Printed and bound in China for Imago

ISBN 978 1 78322 449 4

Visit our website: www.readzonebooks.com

Tall Tilly

by Jillian Powell

illustrated by Tim Archbold

Tilly was growing taller
every day.

She was taller than
all her friends.

She was the tallest girl
in her class.

She was too tall for
her clothes.

She was too tall for her bed.

She was too tall for the bath.

She was even too tall for Ben,
the boy she liked in class!

Worst of all, Tilly wanted
to be a ballerina.

But she was too tall.

Tilly hated it.

She wanted to be small
and dainty, like her
best friend, Molly.

Then Tilly's teacher had an idea.

She made Tilly Sports Captain.

Tilly was so tall that she scored lots of goals for the basketball team...

...and she saved lots of goals for
the football team.

She was so tall she won
every running race.

She jumped the highest high jumps.

She jumped the longest long jumps.

Everyone cheered for her.

Tilly loved being tall after all!